Loving Black Woman

LARRY UKALI JOHNSON-REDD

The Reading Glass Books
(888) 420-3050
www.readingglassbooks.com
fulfillment@readingglassbooks.com

ACKNOWLEDGEMENT

I dedicate this critical thinking text and Black Love spoken word poetry to all the women I have loved all of my life like my mother, aunts, sisters, cousins, in-laws, relatives (Althea Garrett, p.36; Ollie, Lavern, Edwinna and Pearl, p.44; Marion Reed-Brown, p.48; Sharon, Mom, Sandra and Ann, p.76; Patricia Womack, p.90; Shamara and Danellia, p.97; Mom, aunt Quennie and aunt Dorothy, p.108; Darlene, p.109; Ella Womack Gillmore, p.111; and Nakita Curtis, p.121), and girlfriends of the past. I also dedicate this book to my late wife Chinwe, friends of the past and present, and all sisters!

DEDICATION

I dedicate this book to: my friend, the late attorney Cheyenne (Ann) Bell; my poet friends; all the Black women of the world from Papua New Guinea, Australia, south India, Africa, Europe, North, Central and South America, and the Caribbean; Black men who love Black women; Mark Williams, Yaya Fanusi founder of the Conversation On Africa Forum, a group I am working with in the San Francisco area; my original publisher Itibari M Zulu, all people of the world who love liberation, justice and peace, and my next wife! Second Edition of Loving Black Women as an electronic Kindle Book Acknowledgement Page

ACKNOWLEDGEMENT

Loving Black Women was published in 2006 by ARTSP.

Fifty copies or a few were given to family, friends and media and nearly 450 were sold around the USA and the world, Now I am giving the Kindle Book Publishers permission to publish this book of mine "Loving Black Women" in their electronic format only for this second edition. Only Kindle or their paid subscriptions may have access to this book in their electronic format as long as they i.e. Kindle pay me the author appropriate royalties.

Thanks Itibari M. Zulu and Rudolph Lewis!

I Larry Ukali Johnson-Redd, as the author will retain book and audio publishing rights. . The ISBN number is 0-9785772-8-0 for this electronic formatted edition book Loving Black Women. I will publish a completely audio version of Loving Black Women by September 1, 2010. And the 2 CD Set titled LOVING BLACK WOMEN-

Audio will be available through my Journey Books page on Amazon. com at this link:
   http://www.amazon.com/gp/offer-listing/0967422663/ref=dp_olp_1? ie=UTF8&qid=1279781516&sr=1-1-fkmr0

Chicken Bones On-Line Magazine Link:
   http://www.nathanielturner.com/

Journal Of Pan African Studies Link:
   http://www.jpanafrican.com/

TABLE OF CONTENTS

FOREWORD

Well, I have your attention. I hope you enjoy my poetry as I express a little about myself, and how I feel as an African man living in America.

I have a feeling that if you read this foreword you will understand the depth of my feelings through my Black love spoken word poetry. It was once said that if I wrote a book about my love life it would be a best seller overnight. Well this is about as close as we can go in that direction. However, the poetic expressions of a bother say a lot about the brother as well as his essays.

I feel brothers, sisters, and others will learn the best of our essence by reading a book that forms a special trilogy of work that ask about how we understand Africans in America, how African-Americans have been discounted, and how we feel about the modern day challenge of racial discrimination and oppression in a land fertilized by our ancestor's blood. And indeed, fertilized with an American dream, as many of the descendents of the former enslaved remain locked out of chances to advance via the many obstacles erected by white America (some of us face exclusion despite our academic credentials and other efforts of self- improvement).

The golden question in this situation relates to the impact oppression has on the love life and relationships among people of African heritage in America. I hope this book will help to answer that question, as we collectively improve ourselves.

Here are 5 reviews of Loving Black Women by 5 strong sisters. I would like to thank Rudolph Lewis for the originally compiling of these reviews on his Chicken Bones On-Line Magazine. Link:

Reviews by 5 Strong Black Women Of Loving Black Women By Larry Ukali Johnson-Redd Books by Larry Ukali Johnson-Redd/ Journey to the Motherland on sale for $4.oo at Amazon.com / History To Destiny Through Afrocentric Poetry / Loving Black Women on sale for $5.00 on Amazon.com! History to Destiny Through Afrocentric Poetry is out of print!

New Books-Long Distance Love a Memoir about my engagement to a Nigerian Sister and my 2005 trip to Nigeria! I am looking for a new literary agent to present this potential best seller to Publishers! And my newest manuscript titled, American Challenges in the Obama Era!! By: Larry Ukali Johnson-Redd - you guessed it, I need a literary agent who will present this book to Publishers too! Read the reviews and after reading the reviews go to Loving Black Women Part 1 at You Tube.com and check out all 9 clips. Here are 5 Reviews of my book Loving Black Women by 5 strong Black Women! They are Martha Kimbrough, Mukulla Godwin, Pearl Jr., author of Black Women Need Love Too! Cheryl Robinson. Www. JustAboutBooksTalkShow.com and Linda Mayfield-Hayes author of Afroetry; Afrocentric Poetry that Educates! * * * * *

Loving Black Women
WAF RATING:
Larry Ukali Johnson-Redd, Author/Poet Amen-Ra Theological
Seminary Press
Release Date: May 2006 Paperback/2 Audio2CD Set- List
Price: $5.00
ISBN: 0-9674226-6-3

Loving Black Women starts as an essay and the book ends with poetry. The author starts the essay with two basic themes: improving the way African Americans see each other and to have nurturing realistic and wholesome relationships as brothers and sisters. Johnson-Redd goes on to say that this must be done despite racial discrimination, political domination and white supremacy.

Along with preserving the relationship between brothers and sisters, the essay transitions into a global discussion. Here the author begins to suggest that Africans are spread throughout the United States, Caribbean, Central and South America, Saudi Arabia, Pakistan, India and other areas of the Middle East and Asia. Since Africans have a dominant presence around the globe, there should be a dialogue to battle racism, oppression and genocide.

The majority of the essay is a discussion about Black on Black killing. He makes a contrast between the violence that is taking place in the Sudan and what happens in the community where he is from, San Francisco. He suggests that people don't understand the continent of Africa and seldom see Africans conducting modern business in a modern environment. The essay is a great historical and informative overview of what African Americans face in the United States and what Africans endure on the continent of Africa.

After the essay, Johnson-Redd delights the readers with poetry. He has an unquenchable love for the African woman and sees her as the most beautiful creature on earth. He also has wonderful pictures to go along with the poetry. This book is clearly written for those who delight themselves in the beautiful African woman, and it enlightens one on political issues that Africans across the glove have in common.

Martha Kimbrough
WAF Book Reviewer
ORDER NOW

* * * * 2 I Like It (4 Stars): All Ways/Always Loving a Sister! Loving Black Women is a book of poetry offering ideas to improve the many complicated ways that brothers and sisters love each other. It is also a common sense approach to black politics and white supremacy overcoming racial discrimination and political domination. This is a thought-provoking read that enlightens and educates us as a people. Larry is a man who loves his heritage and loves black women! Cheryl Robinson. www.JustAboutBooksTalkShow.com

* * * * 3 Larry Ukali Johnson Redd's book, Loving Black Women left me pleasantly surprised. I was expecting a book of love poems dedicated to black women, but this book is so much more. This compilation of poems also shows a deep love towards motherland Africa and our proud African heritage. I particularly liked: Tribute to All African

xiv

Women, The Beauty of a Sister, I Know You Know Why, and my favorite: Tree of Life part 1 You are The tree of life You are The source of spice You are The carrier of our black seed You are All we really need You are The source of our civilization You are The mother of our Black Nation The world is rough And full of strife But you, you are Our precious tree of life In a time when black women are thought of and categorized in less favorable terms, this book, "Loving Black Women" is a refreshing, and much need change.

Linda Mayfield-Hayes author of Afroetry; Afrocentric Poetry that Educates & Motivates.

* * * * 4 TRUBUTE TO A TRIBUTE Praises are due to Larry Ukali Johnson-Redd's newest literary accomplishment, Loving Black Women." For as an African woman, I am proud of this brother's ability to give explanations as to what removal of black love has inevitably led to, that being self-hate which in turn creates loathing, rejection and violence towards those most like the self. Mr. Johnson-Redd's book should be a must read for those who ask the question, "Why is there so much violence in the Black community?" Mr. Johnson is a true teacher, and instructor of Black life, Black Love. He answers the questions of the causes of self- destructive violence very well when he states in several of his poems/spoken word selections that there is such a pressing need to reclaim love for each other, to heal, to acknowledge our identity as an African people and for the Black man to pay tribute to the Black woman so that unity of mind, spirit and purpose can be achieved, our very survival depends on this. Mr. Johnson-Redd highlights many positive things in his very flowing, easy to read style, which facilitates the comprehension of several essential concepts. These include the need for the African psyche to become whole, that is to eliminate the fragmentation between the male/female psyches caused by the malevolent influence of White Supremacy. He states that: "this white American racism is the most dangerous

force of evil in the world." Yet Mr. Johnson-Redd does not dwell on this premise. Instead, he formulates insights for survival. He yearns for unity within the African Diaspora, and equates love as the foundation for renewing the Black self, family, and nation. His suggestion that there be an 8th and 9th All African People's Congress should be heeded. As an African woman, I can only thank Mr. Johnson-Redd for his respect for and praises to the Black woman. In his expressions of consciousness and gratitude are found hope that we are indeed a people "who can overcome all obstacles.

Mukulla Godwin

* * * * 5 Loving Black Women One night last week, I was having a very tough time falling asleep so I decided to do some reading and the first book on my list was, "Loving Black Women" by Larry Ukali Johnson Redd. I was expecting to read lots of loving poetry, but the book was a lot more. The way the author wrote about the need to collaborate all the African peoples together to develop a movement of Black self-love was so much more than conscious awakening, it was profound enough to allow my fantasies to travel to Africa and be a part of a worldwide solution against White Supremacy that promotes Black unity, which is tied to the end of racism as a form to oppress Black people worldwide. Author, Larry Ukali Johnson Redd is highly educated due to obtaining his formal university degrees, but his intellect went beyond just skimming the surface because he was able to articulate a seemingly complex problem into a few short pages that encourage movement toward solidarity and racial harmony. The poems in this book were so contagious that I read each one of them and when I finished with his emotional and in-touch mastery of the English language, I was able to finally fall asleep, but this time with a smile on my face knowing that someone really loves and values Black women completely, and come to realize that Mr. Johnson-Redd is an

important voice for Black worldwide unity. Pearl Jr., author of Black Women Need Love Too!

*********Larry Ukali Johnson-Redd*********

You are invited to listen to this and join in the conversation and make it a discussion by calling in and participating at 347-215-7831 Remember this segment will begin at 8 PM Pacific Standard Time! Conversations of Africa * * * * *

Books To Mention Review

5.0 out of 5 stars **"...A wonderful soul stirring compilation of poetry ... that enlightens and educates all who have the privilege to read it."**, August 28, 2008

By
Books2Mention Magazine "Editor"
(www.Books2Mention.com) - See all my reviews

This review is from: Loving Black Women (Paperback)

"Loving Black Women is a wonderful soul stirring compilation of poetry uplifting Black Women. It provokes deep thought and demonstrates an appreciation of the African Heritage. Awakening a mixture of emotions as you partake in the author's skillful capacity to fully capture the readers attention."

"Johnson-Redd highlights many issues through out this profound book from Black Love to Black Politics. Loving Black Women is an awesome read that enlightens and educates all who have the privilege to read it."

INTRODUCTION

African culture is matrilineal; something Larry Ukali Johnson-Redd must have known when he composed a work flattering to melanin sisters. It's seldom an African American woman reads a book in praise of herself; however with Larry Ukali Johnson-Redd's latest collection: *Loving Black Women*, this is certainly the case.

I'm not one to blush easily, but the author's sweet lyrics in praise of everything beautiful, everything African and womanly, everything African feminine, is at times overwhelming. Johnson-Redd even uses poetry to teach African men how to attract and keep such beautiful women around.

Now isn't that a twist?

In *Loving Black Women*, Johnson-Redd journeys into a complex subject: African male and female relationships, a topic he appears more than qualified to address given his travels, studies and knowledge of historic context affecting brothers and sisters, often without their knowledge. The author shares this phenomenon briefly in an excellent introductory essay you don't want to miss.

Somewhere along the way… the author seems to have become an expert, an expert in observing how men relate to women, whether they are spouses, relatives, friends or acquaintances. In his book Johnson-Redd shares these observations and where necessary, offers advice.

Loving Black Women is a different way of looking at the complicated nature of relationships: intimate or otherwise.

Johnson-Redd knows success. Maybe it's this optimism and faith in his community to reunite in love, irregardless present dynamics or the seemingly inextricable binds African people allow themselves to participate in which keeps men and women at odds. We are not trapped in these destructive paradigms is a message which shines through Johnson-Redd's text.

No matter how bad it gets... love Black women. The author writes again and again. Between these pages is work praising and loving what is good in African Diasporic sisterhood.

"Loving Black Women" shares the author's hope that other African Diasporic men will realize the loss to humanity when they forget to acknowledge, as Johnson-Redd has: "the beauty of a sister...."

Wanda Sabir (Oakland, California).

Critical Review: Rawsistaz

"Loving Black Women" is a two-fold book about realigning our awareness to improve the way brothers and sisters love each other, and about overcoming racial discrimination, political domination, and white supremacy.

It is Johnson-Redd's strong opinion that African-Americans need to understand Africans in America, to experience nurturing and wholesome relationships despite how African-Americans have been discounted. He elaborates on what he calls the golden question… how much do these oppressive situations impact the _expression of love among people of African heritage in America? He believes that only if we face the future, as a united people will we truly overcome and learn how to express pure love.

With five headers, Brothers and Sisters: Facing the Future Together; African Identity: African World; Sister Praise Poetry; Black Love: Spoken Word and Loving Black Women, he covers a multitude of issues and assertions about life and love. After these indigenous words, Johnson-Redd takes readers on a poetic journey.

Fighting in the Street is a plea for people of color to stop killing each other. No Matter compares and relates the difference or sameness between Tribal war and civil war. Black Love Spoken Word and Loving You All Seasons, challenge brothers and sisters to 'pull up', and learn to embrace each other so as a people we will have a sequel. LOVING BLACK WOMEN is a seed that will hopefully fertilize our dreams as our ancestor's blood fertilized this land, to produce acute awareness and cogent love. This is a concise, thought provoking read that enlightens, educates and embraces us as a people. Reviewed by **Ann** of the Rawsistaz Reviewers (http://www.rawsistaz.com/).

Brothers and Sisters:
Facing the Future Together

This book is about the improving the way we see each other, and the need to overcome racial discrimination, political domination and white supremacy. To reach this level, we need to end 'Black on Black crime' and killing in our community, and around the world (we have lost too many of our young to violence). This means we must work together as Black men and women.

For example, in San Francisco, California there is a struggle for jobs on the $120 million dollar Third Street Light Rail Project and the Hunters Point Shipyard improvements, we need to be actively involved in the process. Most importantly, we need to have the toxins cleaned up in the Hunters Point district of San Francisco that is killing our people.

Second, we need to have nurturing, realistic and wholesome relationships as brothers and sisters despite the obstacles we face with white supremacy and a rightwing tilted government. The quality of our relationships for the love of love should help us overcome the internal and external barriers that stand between us, and our liberation.

In my opinion, the only way we should face the future is as a united people working together despite the challenge of white and Black conservatives who consider our culture and contribution to civilization as insignificant.

Hence, we need make truces and unite our people coast to coast and begin a new love and level of respect that will allow us to work together to make life better.

My strong united brothers and sisters, you are most beautiful and intelligent, wise and brave; your collective strength cannot be denied. Together we can face any challenge. So let us unite like five fingers on a fist so we can survive and thrive.

I now think you are ready to take this journey through the many layers of Black love spoken word poetry in praise of our sisters that also speaks well of our brothers.

I hope you will enjoy this poetic journey, because it 'comes straight from my heart to you.

African Identity: African World

This essay is about African identity throughout the African world because most African people whether in Africa, Asia, American North and South or those in Melanesia have not began an African world conversation to clarify our identity and begin to work together better for common interest.

Never have there been so many African people in the world in so many places, countries and continents. Some of us like the African-Americans or Africans in Europe are residents or citizens in countries where we are the significant minority or just a minority. Yet, many of us remain on the continent of Africa where we are the overwhelming majority; especially in locations called 'Black Africa'.

We also have millions of African people throughout the U.S.A., the Caribbean, Central and South America. Looking east, we see ourselves in Saudi Arabia, Pakistan, India and other areas of the Middle East and Asia. We also have brothers and sisters in Papua New Guinea, the contested western half of the island called West Papua (or even Irian Jaya), a Melanesian or better-stated African people in the Pacific Ocean near the other African populated islands of Vanu Atu, Australia, the Fuji islands, the Solomon islands and other Melanesian islands. Furthermore, West Papua belongs to African people, not the Indonesians whom our African brothers and sisters in the western half of New Guinea feel are racist foreigners trying to take their land.

We need a worldwide African conversation on a governmental and non- governmental basis. A meeting we can call the 8th and 9th All African Peoples Conference, a meeting for Africans to think globally and unite locally as a profound statement on survival itself as we battle racial discrimination, racial oppression, job discrimination, unfair and brutal treatment, genocide, attacks on our African character, our lips, our skin, our youth, and our sisters.

Hence, the independent African countries have to deal with a greedy International Monetary Fund trying to suck all of the debt and interest out of their treasury, leaving little to meet the essential needs of our people.

This factor affects countries all over the world, but causes pain and suffering in African, Caribbean and Pacific Inland countries.

The U.S.A. and Europe lead the IMF, and yet even after the hell and oppression of colonialism and enslavement, the independent African, Caribbean and Pacific nations continue to battle colonial forces in many formations to ensure some freedom and development for our people.

I am throwing out a challenge to Africa's people all over the world to organize an international All African Peoples Congress in Nigeria or Ghana in the next 5 years or less. We owe it to ourselves to continue a world African conversation as African people that can build positive relationships and the discovery of our common problems and to develop programs, positive approaches and solutions to our common problems.

California to Sudan:
Black on Black Killing

We all should be able to see the strength of Africa and African people when our people are united, but much of what we currently see is about the war and genocide (Rwanda, Sudan).

I was born and raised in San Francisco and during the summer of 2004 we have seen a dramatic increase in Black on Black killing by young African- Americans. Some of it has to do with gang wars and ordinary conflict, but the deadly disputes could have been settled peacefully. I say that because in looking at the issues in the Sudan I see elements of disunity the same way I see elements of disunity in the African-American community. Hence, Black on Black crime is a problem we must solve in the U.S.A. and in the international Black community.

In the case of Sudan and other parts of Africa, it is never given a historical context so confusion on the issues in the African-American and general American population remains problematic. Hence very few people know that Sudan is south of Egypt, east of Chad and Nigeria, directly west of Saudi Arabia with borders that touch Kenya and Ethiopia, or that Sudan originally was translated as 'Land of the Blacks'. Notwithstanding, in the history of colonial wars, the people of Sudan gave the British hell in their attempt to invade as the great African Sudanese leader, The Mahdi (the deliverer) led Sudanese armies against the British led by General Chinese Gordon which The Mahdi defeated and in victory planted Gordon's head on a stick.

The U.S. media rarely show Lagos, Nairobi or Accra city life on television, because African-Americans could take great pride in seeing our African brothers and sisters handling modern business in a modern environment.

In contrast, we remember seeing a drought in the Sahel region of North Africa, and again we rarely seen a glimpse of Addis Ababa, Ethiopia, Asmara, Eritrea or the modern urban areas of Nigeria, Senegal, Kenya and Tanzania on American television.

Yet, we do see rare shots of Khartoum, the capital of Sudan, yet only showing a demonstration of Black skinned Africans wearing Arab style clothes demonstrating against any type of foreign intervention. Khartoum is a developed and from what little we could see a Black populated urban area.

In the Sudan context, the west or its media rarely mention the 21-year liberation war fought by the people of south Sudan who are non-Islamic Africans. The Africans of south Sudan fought the central government to an even standstill because they did not want to be ruled by Sharia or Islamic law as promoted by the central government in Sudan's capital of Khartoum.

The western media has been generous in showing us the people of Dafur in the far western province of Sudan, bordering Chad.

The people of Dafur are Black Africans who are Islamic in their religious preference, however we see Black Africans describe how the government of Sudan aircraft and helicopter bomb them as they stood up to the central government and said stop chasing our people out of Dafur by dropping bombs and supplying guns for the Arab militia.

The Sudanese need to get it together and realize that all Sudanese need to be included in the Sudanese family or nation whether from the south, west or north or what ever area of Sudan. Many pro Sudanese government supporters are heard saying they support the Sudanese government, however Sudan like Africans in America are divided. Both the Sudanese brothers and sisters and the African-Americans need to unite, and host a period of national reconciliation.

We African-Americans face a similar but different issue in many urban areas where there are gang or turf wars going on. So while we see the horrific pictures, we know its not an Israeli plot, but rather a true need to share political and economic power fairly among all of the Sudanese (at least that is how it looks from this side of the world).

The African-American populous also needs to get it together and stop fighting among ourselves so we can experience the power of a people. Gang and turf war is problem we face as African people all over. Therefore, we must begin to cool down and end the destructive internal conflicts so we can focus our attention our working together to make things better.

In the Sudanese troubles, we can see our face of division and dissention. We can see the powerlessness and foolishness of Africans not being our brother's keeper. Africans no matter where we come from must rise above destructive action because our internal conflicts only serve the interests of those who oppress us.

In the West we see the stories about wars, refugees running, hungry children and people with AIDS. All of that is a part of the mix in the Motherland, but so is the progress Africa is making.

I cannot remember seeing a positive story about Africa since Oprah traveled there, and even then, Oprah's trip brought attention to suffering - Thank you Oprah for that, but where are the positive or even informative documentaries about Nigeria and other African nations? In addition, I ask myself where are the specials on Ghana? Why keep Americans so dumb about Africa, and those in the African world? What can we do about our situation, will the media in the West do good stories of African progress, and if not what will we do about it?

Today it is becoming obvious to all in the world that the Palestinians are denied statehood as a means of a colonial land grab and political oppression. But how can we Africans be supportive of Palestinians national rights while hearing that Arab militias are killing our African brothers and sisters in Dafur? We should support legitimate national aspirations of the Palestinians. As an act of Arab-African unity, we Africans should call on the Arab League and Arab countries to help counsel Sudan to make peace with all of its regions, provinces and peoples. All the people of Sudan deserve a united peaceful country and an end to oppression.

As much as I want to see the problems settled in the Sudan, I must also look in the mirror and see my brothers involved in deadly internal conflicts in the San Francisco Bay Area. Therefore, I will call for African- Americans all over the U.S.A. to end internal gang wars and realize that in an effort to overcome American racism, we must reclaim our African heritage in America and that is a central aspect of our life and African identity.

African-Americans are making slow and steady progress in some areas of American life like education, government and sometimes even in the job world or corporate world, but we still face an unemployment rate between 25% and 50% in our communities while the white media boasts of an American unemployment rate as a whole as 5% or 6%. Walking around some African-American communities at 2:00pm sometimes seams like Grand Central Station because so many are unemployed.

The lack of private business and commerce on any significant level can be tied to the old KKK practices of targeting successful Black businesses, especially those businesses that competed with white businesses successfully (the KKK targeted black farmers and businesses). The KKK was and still is a white supremacy anti African organization located in the urban and rural areas of America.

Many of us African-Americans are in jail or prison and many of us are victimized by joblessness, homelessness, racial discrimination, stereotyping, racial profiling, police brutality and other aspects of white supremacy. These factors must be discussed when discussing the state of African identity among African-Americans. We have to make our situation clear when we are involved in a worldwide African people's conversation.

Once we understand the historical context and historical answer about why we do not have more private businesses in our communities, even while acknowledging the horrific barriers, historical and contemporary we can indeed overcome those barriers and establish more businesses in our communities as best as we can.

This is a challenge for us: we can make greater efforts to open, support and grow African-Americans businesses. We have to support independent African-American Businesses.

The victory for African-Americans and Africans all over the world is a need to develop African connections and networking that can be utilized to develop businesses and partnerships as well as trading opportunities. Again, we can claim a victory if we overcome the obstacles that others have erected for us, as well as overcome the obstacles we have established ourselves.

We should always assess our potential business partners and ourselves realistically. Our struggle for liberation and development is an essential characteristic of our African identity requiring a united effort and African creativity today and in the future.

As we look at African identity, we must carry our African identity into an analysis of American politics. In the past, African-Americans required several voting rights acts and constitutional amendments like the 14th amendment and a historic national liberation struggle to gain the right to vote. Yet in 2000 the state of Florida headed by Jeb Bush made deliberate efforts unilaterally to deny Black folks and other's their voting rights.

The Florida state police set up roadblocks between Florida African-American communities and their voting places as bold illegal acts of intimidation on Election Day. Through issuing unilateral lists of disenfranchised people without notifying people, it disqualified too many African-American voters, and no effort was spared in steering the election to a George Bush victory.

Florida is not the only state but certainly it was the state most active in disqualifying African-American voting power. So even with the Voting Rights Acts and amendments, the right of African-Americans to vote is still being contested in this so-called American democracy.

Nearly 50 years ago there was a big mess in the country as Emmett Till was killed for whistling at a white woman and the separate but equal system of legal American discrimination was reversed by the U.S. Supreme Court under the international spotlight of Africans all over the world in the process of de-colonization. This ending of legal segregation occurred as part of the Brown vs Board of Education (1954)

Yet 50 years later African-Americans must endure an American educational curriculum that does not include most of the positive contributions that African-Americans have contributed to society. This racism and discrimination makes some African-Americans feel things will never really change as white America continues to attack African- Americans political interests and take Black tax money while only providing less than a fully inclusive educational curriculum.

These factors alienate many of our youth from education, politics and any thoughts of things getting better. These are substantial obstacles. We as African-Americans must overcome these obstacles and obtain the education that prepares us for a future by any means necessary. Working together, we could definitely be more successful in overcoming political, educational and other racist obstacles that white America knowingly and unknowingly erects.

The obstacles and barriers we face are a basic ingredient in our African identity and how we react or respond to those obstacles determines how we move forward, backwards or stand still.

We African-Americans are too strong to let obstacles hold us back, however, why should a country that parades itself as the most democratic country in the world erect such obstacles to hold back the African people they kidnapped and brought to this country at gun point and in chains. Why continue to practice racial and employment discrimination? Why continue to jail and make prisoners at alarming rates? Why use governmental power to take away voting rights of African people that were falsely charged with crimes in many cases? Why do you white Americans allow American police to practice police brutality and even murder African-Americans with impunity and legal immunity? They get away with murder of African- Americans all of the time.

Brothers and sisters around the world ignore the American propaganda you hear and understand the racism, particularly that American style white racism is alive and well and ruling America. This white American racism is the most dangerous force of evil in the world. Living in a racist and unjust system is a challenge, a mighty challenge with huge obstacles; however, we are a mighty strong people.

We African-Americans will make progress despite the obstacles presented by white racism and eventually attain equal rights and justice in the USA by any means necessary.

African-Americans as a part of the world wide African family whole heartedly should condemn the illegal arming of the Haitian opposition and the American supported coup against our brother Aristide, the only legitimately elected President of Haiti (as Colin Powell became a right wing puppet in that illegal effort despite his Jamaican roots; the same can be said for Condolezza Rice). We should salute Hugo Chaves, president of Venezuela for bringing Blacks, Browns and the poor together to defeat the right wing recall effort, and condemn the invasions of Iraq to acquire oil and subjugate the people.

The destiny of African-Americans is in the hands of Africans in America (African-Americans) not George Bush. Our destiny is in our own proud Black hands and we can fashion a path leading to our liberation, education and development. We can overcome every obstacle created by George Bush, white supremacy, and we can overcome obstacles erected in our minds from the scars of enslavement, political oppression, racial discrimination and a low quality education.

What will probably be the most important barrier that we must rise above, as African-Americans is the Black on Black - brother to brother killing going on throughout our African-American communities. If we do not stop killing the best of us, our youth males and females, we will cripple our own efforts to bring progress to our communities and people. We must stop fratricidal brother-to-brother Black on Black killing or we threaten our destiny in a way no other can. This is real talk.

African-Americans as an essential part of the world wide African family should also reach out to Africans, Caribbean's and African Pacific Islanders in a special way as a part of the world wide African conversation. As residents in the USA, we must reach out to each other as African- Americans.

African-Americans should also participate in a world wide African conversation up to and including massive participation in any All African People's Congress in Ghana or Nigeria with in 5 years that occurs. However in our communities we must end the wars among us and unite our efforts to survive and thrive.

The destiny of African identity and African people is in the hands of African People. In particular African-Americans like our Sudanese brothers and sisters are in desperate need of reconciliation nation wide, globally, regionally and locally. We must reconcile ourselves to liberate ourselves.

There is a need to link up with our brothers and sisters who face the Indonesian army in West Papua. There are many areas of the world where we must stop brother to brother killing in the areas of the world where we live so we can work together to put ourselves in a better position to free our selves.

Our precious destiny is in our Black hands so let us do right by our ancestors and our people. Those of us who believe in GOD or Allah, let us be led by a life sustaining way so that the many countries where we have people of various religions unite to preserve our destiny as well as our African identity. Africa and African people must unite as soon as possible.

My Life in Africa

My life in Africa was the most meaningful and eventful time in my life. In the four years I lived in Nigeria (1977- 1981), I cannot count the number of times that a Nigerian walked up to me and spoke their mother language, thinking I was a Nigerian. Other times, I was saluted only because I was an African-American visiting our homeland.

I will never forget the concern for African-Americans expressed by well meaning Nigerians. I will never ever forget the great hospitality the Nigerians as a whole bestowed upon me. I remember the rough edges of some of the bureaucrats I encountered; however, the hospitality of the general population outweighed the challenges posed by some of the bureaucrats. I will never forget the many times I appeared on Nigerian Television in Benin and the beautiful people of Benin City.

Most importantly, African-Americans must know the power of our identity as Africans while we visit or live in our homeland. If you are an African- American and you ever get a chance to visit or live in Africa, I say experience Africa. If you visit Africa, you will feel the unique feeling of African empowerment while living and walking on African land.

More than 400 million Africans around the world must continue this world wide African conversation. The ultimate expression of this worldwide African conversation must be the 8th and 9th All African People's Congress and its local, regional, national and global preparations.

And most important, we must stop the flow of African blood from Black on Black violence locally, regionally, nationally, globally or nothing else may matter.

Sister Praise Poetry

So Much More

We can give
Each other the pleasure
And treat each
Like valuable treasure

Be that virtuous woman
And I'll be your great man
And together we can
Walk through life
Hand in hand

You can be my wife
We can be lovers and friends
As long as we are
the ones that win

We can open that door
And have so much more
WE can make our life
Just like paradise.

Dedicated to
Eseohe Grace Momodu.

Love Is

Love is bittersweet
Knocks one off their feet
Love is like a sugar beat

Don't blame love
For the misery
Don't blame love
For the pain we see
That causes
The world's misery

Do what you can
To make it better
Only goodness will make
The world last forever

Love is strong
Even the mighty see

Love is provided
By our loving God
We can spread love around
Share it and rise
Or let our world down

Love can grow
Between man and wife
Love is the strongest force
In this life.

Love Is Part 2

Love is the simplest
Love is the most complex
Thing in the world
For every man, woman boy and girl
Love is splendid
Love is pain
Love is real
Love is a game
Love is sunlight
Love is rain
Sometimes
Love is a dam shame
A veteran of
One or more of a relationship
I surely know Love is a trip
Look at the sisters
The jazz plays
Just like the
Good old days

You meet a woman
And treat her real nice
She is my sugar
I am her spice

Maybe a day will come
Love is fun

Maybe after awhile
You are on the run

Tons of ladies
In this happy hour tonight
Ladies look good
And the perfume smells right
Look at the girls
Watch their moves
African-American sisters rule
While the brothers drool

There is
Love at a glance
Look deeper it maybe a trance
Or a bad chance
Looking for the love
The one that will stick
Love is best I bet you
When love sticks like glue
Love is daylight
Love is night
If you find a real love
Maybe, carefully take a bite.

This poem was written at the Phillip R. Bell First Friday Happy Hour at the Spot Light On The Square in Alameda, CA in early May 2001.

Tight Jeans

Tight Jeans, tight meat
Tough Jeans look so sweet
Really tight jeans you know what I mean
Designer Jeans with busting seams

Walking down the street
Look so good to those who see
You got two patches on your hips
And pretty pointed tips.

Tight jeans with a pretty Black Face
Moving with rhythm and grace
Tight jeans cuffed at the base
Tight thighs, with no free space

Tight Jeans on Black Queens
Designer jeans with busting seams
Looking so sweet
Tough jeans with busting seams

Dedicated to Nigerian (Spinsters)
young adult women I saw in Nigeria wearing tight jeans.

Pretty African Lips

I want to kiss you
But I can't
I want to touch you
A reality it may seam
But that's only a dream

A whole continent away
Wished I could touch you
The first thing this day
Yet you are far way

I want to kiss your lips
I wonder about you
From your laps, thighs and hips
I really want to kiss
Your pretty lips

So I'm writing this poetry
Stirred up by your picture
Thinking of your pretty lips
Wondering about your pretty hips

Get Through

I tried to call
You are not here
If your were here
This is what
I would say dear

I love talking to you
Longing for us to be near
In love
But distance I fear

What I really want
Is to bring you near
My beautiful dear
Can you hear?

Tried to call
But I couldn't get through,
This is what I would
Say to you

God Will Make a Way

Go will make a way
I will unite with a wife
soon one day
and we'll be on our way

Don't rush
the land is lush
open the door
of a blessing in store

She will be nice
And very sweet
She will be
The real deal

Soul sister Black Queen
And I'll be
her Black king

And the day will come
We'll unite as one
We'll live together
Live life and have fun

Eye Candy in Atlanta

The girls and women
Are so pretty
In this
Chocolate city

So many pretty smiles
Dressed in the latest styles
And the sisters are very intelligent
Talking to a sister, is time well spent

In a city
That Blacks rule
And many folks
Go to school

And all the
Pretty faces
In so many
different places

On the streets
Clubs and malls
See pretty intelligent women
Not just pretty dolls

In the home of Coca Cola
And even Fanta
See all the eye candy
In the sisters of Atlanta

Tribute to All African Women

Some think
We're not it
Some think
We're not up to it

This is a tribute
To all Black Women
You've always been
Our very best friend

Sharing our identity
Walking with us through history
Walking out of slavery
Sharing our destiny

This is a tribute
To all African Women
You've always been
Our very best friend

Together we are family
We are not enemies
We are together
Like birds and bees

Every time we spoke
We are the same folk
You are the best lovers
For me and my brothers

Never ever forget
Please unite us together
All of us
Are sister and brother

This is a tribute
To all Black Women
You have always been
Our very best friend

You are
a work of art
You are
Queen of our heart
You are
The roots we need
You are
The pillar of our creed

This is a tribute
To all African Women
You have always been
Our very best friend.

We Are Together

African Man
My Brother, My Friend
African Woman
My Sister, My Kin

One aim, one destiny
We struggle in unity

African people
We are together
Brothers and Sisters
United forever

Down with exploitation
of our life and soul
We stand together
The young and the old

Down with our foes
Apartheid and Jim Crow
Down with colonial mentality
And that of the Negro

Scattered we stand
On many a land
The Black Woman
The Black Man

African people
We are together
Brothers and Sisters
United forever.

The Beauty of a Sister

When you see her walking
WHEN YOU SEE HER TALKING
Let me tell you mister
That's the beauty of a sister

Think about her wit
Check out her mind
What you will find
Our sister is one of a kind

Like a hurricane
Stronger than a twister
Strength and integrity
Is in the beauty of a sister

Walking with us through history
Sharing with us our destiny
Like a sun, no the moon
She is covered in mystery

So many shades of beauty
To our race, a sense of duty
In so many shapes
A sister's beauty escapes
And that is a shade
That never ever fades

Let me tell you mister
She's stronger than a twister
Stand up! If you agree with me
On the beauty of a sister

Please do not bleach her
Please do not mistreat her
Talking to you my brother
About the beauty of a sister

She's rough dainty and sweet
She's balanced on her feet
I'm not talking about a twister
But the beauty of a sister!

My Dream

My dream is for Black Kings
My dream is for Black Queens
My dream is to unify the Black Nation
My dream is for Black Liberation

The order is given for an attack
Divided we cannot do anything
United we can drive them back

We are despised in this land
Unite Black minds I know we can
Come on Black woman
Come on Black Man

The healing power of love
Is what we are made of?
Keep it warm not cold
Let it flow from our inner soul

My dream is for beautiful black cream
My dream is for beautiful Black queens
For strong black kings
For pretty black genes
For more Black Cream
MY DREAM, MY DREAM, MY DREAM.

The Faces of Africa

There are many faces
Of the Motherland
Faces of the Black Man
Faces of the Black Women

The faces of Ethiopia
And even Nigeria
Sweet faces in Atlanta
Pretty faces in Tanzania

Many beautiful smiles
Many beautiful shades
I'm really talking about
The faces of Black babes

Don't forget my Jamaica
Tobago and Trinidad
And there are a few more
That I must add

Beautiful Black faces
In the Republic of Fuji
Beautiful black faces
In Papua, New Guinea

Beautiful African faces
Around San Francisco Bay
A beautiful face flying next to me
Flying to LA.

Black Woman, You are a Poem

I saw you on United Airlines
I saw you homeless in San Francisco
Another time in Chicago, you said
Your red black and green is live not dead

Most appreciated Black Woman
Though disrespected by some
To me my sister
You are number 1

We are nothing without you
We are whole with you
Cause you can be real
And that we can feel

You are our rhythm and soul
You are our rhyme
You are our future's producer
Making history and the future in our time

You are our beauty and
You are our survival
Please don't leave a Black man
For any other rival

Cause you are our soul
Our future continuation
Mother of our Black Nation
Work with us for liberation

And you are our compliment
Reflect us like the moon
Stick by us
And we will obtain our liberation soon

Because though we are
Not quite what we should be
Held back and oppressed by white society
You and I are one entity

Black woman you are a poem
you are black history in motion
We really love you
With all of our real devotion

And though we are not free
Or all we want to be
We cherish your company
And love and appreciate you totally.

I Know You Know Why

Sweet as a pretty flower
Something sweet has gone sour
There is no need to cry
When it ends, we say bye-bye

One tear may fall, from her eye
There is no need to cry
So many relationships die
I know you know why

You got to do your thing
What we had was only a fling
There is no pain only a sting
You are free to do your thing

I know you know why
I said good-bye

My Beautiful Wife

I want to
See eye to eye
With you
I want to see
What you see
I want you
To see what I see

Eye to eye
Nose to nose
Lips to lips
Love to love

I want to see
You yesterday
Today
And tomorrow

Like a bright
Sunny day
I want you to
Come my way

My African queen
Brand new thing
My beautiful new wife
For the rest of my life

Written 10/24/03 10:30pm

Tree of Life
Part 1

You are
The tree of life
You are
The source of spice

You are
The carrier of our black seed
You are
All we really need

You are
The source of our civilization
You are
The mother of our Black Nation

The world is rough
And full of strife
But you, you are
Our precious tree of life

Part 2

Black Women
Is my tree of life?
My mothers and sisters
My aunts and aunties

Black Women
Tree of life
You're the lovers
Of me and my brothers

Stand by us
In this white supremacy world
Though we may not say enough
We need you Black Women/girl

Jet Ride with a Sister

She has soft looking
Beautiful Black skin
The kind you look at
And wish you were touching

Wrapped in braided hair
The white boys dare to stare
Exotic Black
You want to attract

She sits there
Listening to her CD
We talk a little
She is spoken for, not for me.

Continuously

Loving you
In the morning
That is just
How it is

Loving you in
The afternoon
Hoping to
See you soon

Loving you
Day and night
Loving you
And knowing it is right

Continuously
You and me
Continuously
In love you see.

Love Your Flavor

I like your flavor
It's you I savor
To the last drop
Love you, can't stop

Love your flavor
When it is cold
Love your flavor
When it is hot

Love you when
We are together
Love you when
we are apart

Love you when
When you do me a favor
Let me love you
And enjoy your flavor.

Black Love Spoken Word

Breathing While Black

One day
a brother was arrested
for breathing
while Black

A sister
was arrested
for driving
while Black

Too many times
It's just like that
When our folks are arrested
for breathing while Black

Ahmadu Diallo
Murdered and
that's a fact
Because one morning
he was walking while Black

We all know
Someone
We know it's
a fact

Arrested for
No good reason
Driving while Black

And a Haitian Brother Louima
Was subjected to an attack
Assaulted with a stick
Living while Black

Another brother is
about to be jacked
and his only crime
Breathing while Black

Walking while Black
Talking while Black
Running while Black
Thinking while Black
Driving while Black
Working while Black
Living while Black
Breathing while Black

Breathing While Black II

It is really something
To be Black
A misguided brother looks at you
Look out for an attack
Breathing While Black

The boys in blue
Profile you
Cause you are Black
You better hold back
Or prepare for an attack
You know if you're
Breathing While black

You been exploited, you been jacked
You know if you're, Breathing While Black
Beating that brother with a stick
You don't care, what you split

The blue boys beat, the brother to death
The brother is dead, when life is wealth
Open you eyes, to the fact
We are Breathing
While Black

*Dedicated to the memory of our brother beaten to death
on national TV in Cincinnati, OH*

No Good for the Oppressed

Struggle on for progress
You must try
Your very best
Push up together
To pass the test
The test is survival
Facing brutal opposition
Unity is the solution
In face of prosecution
Because oppression
Is no good for oppressed
And no good for the oppressor

No limit to what
We can do
If we work together
United through and through
Do the best we can
For the Black Woman
And Black Man
Discrimination is
No good for the oppressed
And no good for the oppressor

Stay united in George Bush land
Work together we
Know we can understand the call
United we stand
Divided we fall
Please do not ignore the call
Repression is no good
For the oppressed
No good for the repressor

Florida Nights

We got Florida fights
And voting rights
Our ancestors were
Hung days and nights
For registering to vote
And pole taxes
When you study
The facts and
vote but please do more
Pull up our people
Who are treated unequal
No more days
Or Florida nights
Highjacking
African voting rights
In Florida, Ohio or Michigan
In Detroit, Miami or Muskegon
Too many bled
Too many dead
Told to get
Too many told to get
Out of town
Before sundown
Just because we wanted
To vote
Vote for president
And vote for Black Liberation
Vote for freedom
Of the Black Nation

Vote for our
Ancestors
Vote down their barriers
Vote for our
Reparations
Vote for our interests
Africans
But make sure
you organize
So we can rise

A Poem for My Mother

My mom is love
From God above
Tough, compassionate, soulful
Spiritual love
My mom gave me
The ultimate gift
And so many ancestral gifts
And when my head was bowed
So many inspirational lifts
When I was young
Mom gave me knowledge
And wisdom
Mom also gave me
A part of God's kingdom
And mom gave this love
To all seven of us
And never complained
About the burdens of us
And is loved by all of us
You can look
At all seven of us
And see mom's beautiful hand,
Tough and sweet.
African-American Women
From North Little Rock,
Arkansas (Tie plant area)

Mom you are my roots
My connection to my past
My link to our African ancestor
And giver of my future
Because with no past,
There is no future
Momma, you are God's gift
To all seven of us.

Momma's73rd Birthday Card-Poem

What can I
Give to you
On your
73rd birthday
Today I could give
You a song
Or I could
Give you a poem
How ever
You gave us life
As a great mother
And a great wife
This is my call
You can't beat life
that you gave us all
Happy 73
To you mommy
Happy 73
To you mommy
Happy 73
To you mommy
Happy 73
To you mommy

Tribute to Our Family

I remember
Trips by car
To Los Angeles
And our dad buying
All seven of us hamburgers
NEVER A HUNGRY DAY

I remember
Taking a bath in a bucket
In the shower of the
Old projects in 1960
At south Ridge road and La Salle
Hunters Point San Francisco
And playing with Jerome Fell

I remember
Moving to Lakeview in 1961
We were happy to move
Into a house at 38 Brighton Avenue
And jumping from
A table red
And landing on
Our strong steel framed bed

This is a tribute
Top my family
Live on in unity

We are colorful
And many shades of Black
And true diversity

Rooted in love
True respect
United in our destiny

Can our Mom's
Tender care
Cease towards the
Child she bears

In our family
Mom's love will
Always be there
And our late Daddy Redd
We all remember
What he said
Family comes first
Through the best
And through the worst

When Dad died
We united and cried
What a tragedy
For our family
But Dad had to transcend
And go on to heaven
While we continued
To love GOD and life
And our family
And we survived!!!!

No More Fighting in the Street

In 2004, no more
Fighting each other
Fighting in the street
It's your own people you beat

Young people, preteens
And teens
On the ground, beating down
Each other, sister and brother

Can we resolve conflicts
With our licks and hits
Can we love each other
Can we be sister and brother

Remember they are
Looking at us
Brown, Red White and Yellow
Among us, keep it mellow

Antioch's Lone Tree
Between Long's and Rite Aide
Blacks fighting hand to hand
Is the shame of Blacks in this land

Even our little girls
No fighting each other
Little boy/ little girl
Instead prepare
To rule our world

Bring about a better day
Resolve issues another way
Put your sites
On fighting for our rights

In 2004
Fight no more
Get it together
Close that door

Prepare yourself
Seriously in school
Prepare boy and girl
So we can rule our world
Prepare boy and girl
So we can rule our world.

*Dedicated to African-American teens and preteens
in Antioch, California*

No Matter

Black Folks
No matter where
You are
We don't need
Tribal war
Some have civil war
But we are dieing
From tribal war
No matter where we are
If you're Black
You are a star
We don't need
To die anymore from
gang or tribal war
But the warriors need
jobs and hope or
paid job training
Just to cope
So we got to
Make it better
For young folk
Talking to the older folk
Cause we don't
Need more
Tribal war
No matter where we are
We don't need gang war
No matter where we are
We don't need tribal war
No matter where we are

Love in the Neighborhood

Love in the Neighborhood
Love or it is no good
One love Black Love
In the hood
Between neighborhoods
Or life will be no good

Love Fillmore
Love HP/ BV
Love in Lakeview
One love in the hood
One love or its no good
Do not be ill
Black Love is needed
on Portrero Hill Love in the neighborhood

Black Love or Black Death
Make up your mind
One love for our kind

There won't enough
Brothers for every sister
If the killing
Don't stop mister
Brothers got the power
To make it stop
Or we'll see
Another brother drop
Don't shoot a brother

Don't make a brother fall
And stand in his blood
What happened to "one love"
Brothers got the power
To make the shooting stop
Calling on the brothers
On every block
Cause what is happening
To murdered brothers mothers
Wives and sisters
Sons and daughters
The power to make it
Stop, stop, stop
Is in the hands
Of brothers
on every block

I turned on the news and heard that a 27 year old Black resident was killed on Portrero Hill in a shoot out, involving more than 40 bullets fired 6/22/04. So, I call on San Francisco youth and all African-American youth to stop the killing especially in our communities

Love Thang

It's not about your name
It's not about your game
To continue killing each other
Is a dam shame

It 's not about lust
But warfare between us
It's a love thang we need
To nurture and grow our seed

It's about
One love
Change the game
To a real love thang!

We got to
Change the game
We got to know
It's a love thang

We can't wait
Till the hate
Is too great
Cause then it's too late

Get it going now
It's a love thang
Change the game
It's a love thang

Use common sense
Cause it's too tense
Stand up
In our people's defense

No more Black bloodshed
Not while we are underfed
No more shooting

No more brothers dead
Black on Black love
Is the name
Black on Black Love
It's a love thang.

Black on Black Love
Not black on black war
Black on Black Love
Where ever we are

Black on Black unity
Not just to rhyme
It's a love thang
In this our time

Black on Black love
Your time or mine
Change the game
It's a love thang

Reach Into Yourself

Look inside nowhere else
You'll find a pot of gold
Wisdom of ancestor's of old
Knowledge of God's Power
Unsold and untold
Stay true to yourself
And our mighty people
Make and enhance Black Life
Don't be a part of our demise
Reach into our gold mines
Historic truth, wisdom and rhymes
Use good common sense
Reach Into your soul
Reach into our ancestor's fold
Find Solomon's Mines of Gold
Wise up with ancestral wisdom
In these times
Reach into your inner-self.

Rain

Why do we
Make blood run
Like a pouring rain
Why do we cause families pain

Why do we stand?
In each others BLOOD
If we from
The good BLACK MUD

Shooting in our community
Another brother fatality
Killing off brothers
In our community
What about longevity?

And unity
In our community
While we share one destiny
We kill each other
Like an enemy

And where will
lovely sisters
select a man
If there no more of
the young Black Man?

Taking it
From the very top
Brothers we got
To make it stop

One brother killed
By a crazy cop
Other brothers killed
Right on the block

Like a bomb
It goes tick tock
But my brothers
Make it stop

My people
It's got to stop
My brothers
It's got to stop

The mothers say
It's got to stop
Our sisters say
It's got to stop

Real Black Love

I am in awe
Of the power of

My Black Women
So happy my Sisters
We are Kin
So happy my Sisters
You are apart of us
May Love thrive among us
Respect each other
And, no one cuss
May GOD Bless
All positive Black Love

Respect is
What Love is made of
Life can't stay the same
So we have to make change
We have to love ourselves
Take Love off the shelves

So my sisters
We are Kin
So happy my sister
My real good friend
So happy you are
Apart of us
May Love thrive
Among us
May Love flourish
Among us
May Love grow
Among us
May Love be
Our friend

May we always
Share a blessed love
May we always fit
Like hand and glove

If you feel it
Bring it home
If you feel it
Say right on

Wear the Crown Again

Let's go back
In time in our mind
When you and I
Wore the African crown

You know we need to
Wear the crown
In your city or town

And as you wear
Our pride filled crown
Don't act like a fool
or a clown

Wear the crown again
With love and pride
Wear the crown again
When you walk or ride

Wear our proud
African crown
Don't kill a brother
In your city or town
Wear our proud
African crown
Even if you live
In a rural area
not in a town

Please don't kill
A brother or a sister
Cause they too
Wear our crown

We can all
Get along
And sing
a unity song

Then we will survive
And we will thrive
And until all of our freedom comes
We will stay alive

So keep our pride
And wear our crown
Don't fight against each other
in your city or town

*Dedicated to Participants of 13 Annual Africa/Diaspora Conference
Sacramento, California May 1, 2004*

The Definition of African

Our World Wide Conversation

I am African
Africa, Brazil, New Guinea
West Papua, Fuji, Cuba
Jamaican, Trinidadian, Guyana
Venezuela

If you are a Black Man
Or Black Woman, You are African
Some in New York, Some in Canada, Some in Honduras
Some in Florida, Some in England, Some in Nicaragua
Some in Frisco, Some in Spain, Some in Panama
Some in Los Angeles, Some in Germany, All in Van Autu
Uniting with All Caribbean's

All African-Americans
All Cape Virdians
All Beleizians
All Haitians
All Africans are we
All Africans are Black, link it up!

Loving Black Women

Greetings to a Sister

Hello my beautiful sister
Whatever your name
You are Black and beautiful
And we share fame

Hello my beautiful sister
I have no doubt
There's something about you
That knocks a brother out
Whether or not

I know your name
I will say hello
Cause we share
African fame

You I must respect
You I must protect
Cause we share fame
I'll never call you
Out of your name

There are good brothers
Don't paint us all bad
Sharing love and respect between us
Is the best we ever had!!

Hello my sister, what is your name?
Hello my sister, A greeting not a game
Hello my sister, African fame
Hello my sister, Is a unity thang
Hello my sisters!!!!

Speak Jazz Please 1

Speak Jazz please
Love the notes you squeeze
Speak from your very soul
Speak jazz please

Play jazz please
Cause we are being squeezed
Play from your very soul
Get down please don't tease

Brother play that horn
All nightlong
Blow the notes
That contains our hopes

Play the base
Reflect our race
The pain on our face
Place jazz with grace

Play jazz 400 years
Play for all our tears
Play jazz for you and me
And years and years of fears

Like a warm summer breeze
Like a Black women's squeeze
Like the birds and the bees
Speak jazz please!

Speak Jazz Please Part 2
Written for African-American History Month 2001

Like a warm
Summer breeze
Like a beautiful
Black woman's squeeze

You can do it hard
Or do it with ease
Horn player don't tease
Speak Jazz Please

Speak and let
Them know
Play Jazz
Low as you can go

Play from the depth
Of our very souls
Like roots, breathe
Through the tall trees

Play Jazz like
Those tall African Trees
Play for our people
Rising from our knees

Play Jazz 3/5ths of a human being
For four hundred years of captivity
And one hundred years
Of trickery where they said
We were free
But we knew, not really

Play for our souls
Play hot let it glow
When you let it go
Play like hot coals
Play so we will grow
Play cause we are to go
For freedom in this century
And attain true liberty

Play Jazz please
Like a warm summer breeze
Play Jazz please
Like a Black Woman's squeeze

Soul Truth

I love your
Dark deep tone
And your light brown skin
Really turns me on

Love your
Hazel to dark eyes
Love your curves
And historically close ties

Love to see you while
I'm walking down the street
Really love to see you
Even if we do no speak

Dark and lovely
Light and out of sight
And every sister in between
Know what I mean

Sister you are
Sweet and tight
One race, one destiny
You know that's right

Springing from
A common root
Black Women are beautiful
And that's the soul truth

Millions of Black Women

Millions of Black Women
With us on the ship
Millions of Black Women
Together we made the trip
Millions of Black Women
Fine, beautiful and intelligent
You are heaven sent
We can share a house
Or even a tent
Millions of Black Women
of African origin and decent
Millions of sisters
Stand by their Black Man
On African, Caribbean
Pacific and American Land
Throughout the African World
From the woman to the girl
Millions of beautiful sisters
Assisting the Black Man
Brothers love our sisters
The best way you can!!
Brothers say it loud
We love you
And my sisters
We need you too

Home Alone

Home alone is no fun
When you are all alone

The music is on
No conversation
No motivation?
No action?

Love yourself
Before you love
Someone else

Work hard
to achieve success
Do your very best
Work hard and achieve success

But you can't forget
You are home alone
Call someone
On the phone

If you must
What about lust
In a lonely home
When you are all alone

For The Sisters

For the sisters
Standing strong
My love
Is old and long
Working with us
Through our misery
Laying with us
Throughout history
The good sisters
Let their goodness shine
Your sisters and mine
For the sisters
I got much respect
Cause without them
We are a wreck
Every sister
is a mother
Love and respect
From every brother
And when it
Comes to the heart
A sister gives you
A brand new start
And when times
Are really hard
She gives nourishment
And encouragement

For the sisters
No neglect
For our sisters
For real respect
For the sisters
Throughout history
To the sisters
Salutes from me
And if you
Agree with me mister
Hugs and kisses
For the sister
Cause she doesn't
have to accept our kisses
she can choose to be miss
or they can be our Mrs.
We must earn their trust
It's more than lust
There is something real
inside of us
Love sisters to the heart
And to the bone
And to the sisters
Stay strong!!!!!

Love Poem

This is not a poem
But a love song
As the rain falls
I wish I could
Hear your calls

Yet you are
Too far away
To hear me
Reach out to you today!

Then comes the night
Delta thunder and light
This is not a song
This is a love poem

Feel you coming on
Very soon you'll be home
And I will see your face
Here in this place

So far away
Wish you were here
Wish you were here
Closer to me my dear

Remember this is no song
This is a love poem
Wishing you were here
Closer my sweetie dear!

A long distance love affair
Is a love so deep to share
Closer my sweetie dear
Wish you were hear

Picture This

Picture this
She's an African Queen
And she shows it
She's a Black Woman
And I know it
Picture This
We lived in
History's Huts
And pulled ourselves
Out of Oppressive Ruts
Emerging smooth and Cool
And smart, no fool
Only calling you a Queen
My beautiful Sister
Too much respect
You, I must protect
Picture This
Walking Arm and Arm
Recognize your Charm
Both of us
In it together
Both of us
Sister and Brother
And if you can
Picture This
Then my folks
Make us a new reality

A permanent
Sister/Brother
Praise Poem
And lose
Our negative reality
Picture This
My people

Imagine That

Imagine That
You are Proud
And Black
Imagine That
You go to Africa
And you come back

Imagine That
You are treated
Like a King or Queen
And that is a fact

Imagine That
There is Unity
Among all that's Black
And Black on Black crime

There is none of that
No disrespect
For our sisters
No murder of
Our brothers
And elders are respected

And our rights
We work together
So our rights
Are protected

Imagine That
My Fellow Black

Looking Good

Just like
My favorite food
My sisters are
Looking good
Good sisters and brothers
In a real mood
Sisters looking real good
Hey brothers
Be it understood
The sisters, looking good
When they do
What they should
Sisters are looking good
Like good smooth
Black Ebony wood
Our sisters are
Looking so good

Dedicated to the brothers and sisters (1200+) who attended and graduated from San Francisco State University during the 2004 Black Graduation that celebrated 180 new African-American graduates. Please note that there was no white media openly present because there was no drive by shooting. I received my second Masters degree that day.

Good Intensions

I think good of you
My lifelong partner
Woman I love you
Black Woman,
Cause it's you
Always there
For me
The best part
Of we
If you love me
Like you should
You better believe
It's all good
Good intensions
For you
Love is all
A Black Man like me
Wants to do
For you
Nothing but
Good intensions
No tension
Good intensions
No tension,
Good intensions

Black Togetherness

Black Woman
Supreme Attraction
I give you
All my attention

Black Queen
My Black Dream
Go Ahead
Exotic queen

We applaud your
Black loveliness
Can we share additional
Black togetherness

Be who you are
Truth is you are
A Beautiful
Black Star

Looking ahead
To our destiny
I am happy our
Destiny is unity

To our Black sisters
To our Black Queens
Working together
We'll achieve our dreams

Celebrate
Our Blackness
With more
Black Togetherness

And to my brothers
On the scene
Don't you just love!!
A real Black Queen

It is all righ
Treat our sisters right
If it is on
Then say right on

In My Mind

Although you are
A total stranger
You are so beautiful
Like trouble-danger

I look at you
In your face
I watch you move
With your grace

Looking at you
Puts me in
A special place,
Shall I give chase?

Can you be so fine?
And yet still normal,
I ask and you say
I am normal

Then I recover
Once I discover
I am in a strange town
With fine ladies all around

And the music
Is turned on
And I imagine
A fine lady in a song

Then I return
To my reality
I am sitting here
All alone

Pay Attention

She has been
With Us Since
The Beginning of Time
And Lovers of Your Brother
And Mine
Isn't It Time
We Pay Attention
Sharing a Hut
With Us, Like Us
Made From Black Dust
Fresh and Clean And
The Subject of Our Lust
Not Just A Woman
But Our Black Woman
An Old and New
Invention
Respect Her
And Pay Attention
Not Talking
Dissention
My Brother
Pay Attention
And Every time
She Looks So Fine
Sisters of Mine
It's Your Love
We Must Find
In Our Mind
Understand Trust
Respect You Must

Feel the Power
In The Thrust
God's Original`
Holy Invention
No Pretension
Togetherness
Is common sense
Why love 50 percent
When you can
Love 100%
Pay Attention
My Sister and
Brother
Pay Attention

Dedicated to all Black women and men.

Dialog with the Black Woman Part 1

I want you
I need you too
Naturally
Black and Proud
So I can
Shout it out loud
About the love
I found in you
Because you are
Sweet and lovely too
Better than Mountain dew
With you
I'll never be through
I am for you
And my sister
I love you too
And all I can do
Is think about the love
I have for you
Love my beautiful
Black Woman
Come out of my dream
Bring on your beauty and steam
Make me warm
All over
Be my lucky leaf clover
Be my life long lover
Through the ups and downs
Show me you'll
Always be around

Then I will know for sure
It's your endless love I found
And it's sound
I want you
And need you too
Be Black and Proud
So I can
Shout it out loud

Some More Dialog with a Black Woman #2

We've been
Fussing and fighting
cause you look
Somewhere else
Truth is I want you to myself
Too much beefing
About this and that
Too much beefing
Like dog and cat
Do we have
To beef
about this or that
until we get the love back
Can we stop
Fussing and fighting
Can we talk
About good loving
Tell me where
You come from
Tell me
I am #1
Tell me you
Down for me
Tell me you think
Of us as we
I'll ask you
What are we
Fighting for
I'll ask you
Can you close that door

If you listen
I'll tell you more cause
we really need each other
Is love worth fighting for?
Can we close that door
And love each other
Some more
And love each other
Some more
and love each other
some more
and when you say
you want no more
we will cuddle
and feel the
Afterglow

Black Woman of Mine
Dialog with a Black Woman Part 3

Since the beginning of this time,
Black Woman of mine,
You're always on my mind,
When you are loving and kind,
Sweeter than the sweetest wine
Soft and cuddly,
Light or dark and lovely,
Putting up with me
Making us we

Black Woman of Mine
Dialog with a Black Woman Part 3 continues

My apologies
For misguided brothers,
Maybe we be your best lovers,
Because we need you,
Way more than any others.
Like the queen of Sheba,
And still you're so fine
Sweet Black Woman of mine,
Since the beginning of time,
My sister Sweet,
Black Woman of mine
Not just to rhyme
You are always
On my mind
Down the line since the
Beginning of time
You have
Always been so fine
Black sweetie of mine
May we see
The future together
May we be together forever
Black woman of mine

We are two
In this journey
From our history
On to our destiny
For all time
Black woman of mine
You are always, always, always
On my mind.

Woman of My Dreams
Dialog with a Black Woman Part 4

You are
The woman of my dreams
You are a queen among queens
And the most beautiful thing
I want to give you my ring

You are the girl of my dreams
I want to make
You my queen
I can talk to you
On the phone

But I want you
In my home
Sweet Woman
In my dreams,
I want to bust the seam

So I can become your King
So you can be my queen
So you can emerge
From my dreams
And be my real Queen.

Love Me True

Love me true
And I'll
Never be
Through with you

From the first
Day I see you
The first time
I kiss your face

I'll pay attention
And love you too
I'll never be
Through with you

I promise
To hold you tight
I will always
Treat you right

I will love
Getting to know you
Looking in your eyes
and close, close ties

Sharing my world
Respecting your
point of view
really getting to know you

Love me true
And I'll
Never be through with you

Loving Black Women

Your beauty
Is legendary
Sweeter than the
Sweetest berry

For as long
As we remember
You have our child
Please deliver

When you were made
God did a good thang
I was so happy
I sang

And thanked
our maker
and then we begged
Please never take her

Since that day
What can I say
We have been understand
Loving our Black Woman

Loving our Black Woman
For standing by us
Love for our Black Women
From the Black Man

Loving our sister
For standing by us
Loving our Black Woman
Loving you is a must!

Love the Black Woman
For the love
She is giving
While she is living

Giving you flowers
while you are living
we appreciate
The love you're giving

Loving beautiful
Black Women
Sister understand
This is the love of a Black Man

The Blacker the Berry

The Blacker the Berry
The sweeter the juice
There is nothing
like A Black Woman
And that is the truth
From her brains
to her tone
My love for
The Black Woman
Goes on and on
There is nothing
like a Black woman
And that is the truth
A sister's got the love
And a sister has the fruit
Don't you ever forget
A sister's got our roots
The Blacker the Berry
The sweeter the juice
Asian sisters are fine
Latina sisters are cool
But our sisters
Make us drool
The Blacker the berry
The sweeter the juice
A sister has our fruit
And our genetic roots

Cause a sister got the motion
Like a hypnotic potion
Like waves on the ocean
In hot hot oils or lotion
The Blacker the berry
The sweeter the juice

Black Love Spoken Word

Black is the love
We must give
If we are to survive
If we are to live

Black is the love
In our spoken word
Love is first
Second and third

Black Love my people
So we can pull up

Black Love my people
So we can pull up
Black Love my people
So we can have a sequel

Black Love is a matter
Of life and death
Black Love or
Breathe your last breath

Black Love cause
It is better than
Beating down your own
Black Woman or Black Man

Black Love cause
Our Black Woman
And Black Man
Really need it

Black Love cause
We will live with it
Black Love cause
We will die without it

Black Love is our
Spoken word
First, second
And third

Black Love Spoken Word
Like Black Love incense
Black Love is
Common sense

Love Your Smile

I live to smile
At you Black Woman
I am your
Black Man

Daytime
or night
You are beautiful
In my sight

Cause we come
From one seed
My Black Woman
You are all I need

Through hard times
And all my rhymes
You are my sunshine
All of the time

I look at you
My sister and smile
For you, I'll walk
A country mile

to see the sunshine
for awhile
in your
beautiful smile

smiles and hugs
soothe the lonely
smiles and hugs
soothe the homely

When a smile
Is really done
Give it
A rerun

because smiles
And love
Is like hand
And glove

Cause we are weak
When we are divided
We are strong
When united

I look at you
Across the way
You smile at me
And make my day

Smiles from dark and lovely
From light and out of sight
Smiles from our sisters
Make a bad day right!!

Relationships

When a sister shows
She is down for you
You better know
What to do

Respect her and
Treat her right
Show your sensitive side
And cruise with her tide

Build it up
But very slowly
When the time is right
Step to her boldly

Loving a sister
Is very complicated
To do it right
You must be dedicated

Lay your cards
on her table
she will tell you
if she is able

No fuss, no rush
Make a sister blush
Love her if you can
Or if she says you must

Emotions are serious
With lust you only play
A relationship
Can not be made a day

Take it easy
Grow tender love
To make it
Fly like a peaceful dove

If it is right
You will know
Love will fit like
A hand in a glove.

Loving You All Seasons

We will do our thing
I will love you
Throughout the spring
I will love you
Throughout the summer
Like a long distance runner
When it is hot
Love is the tool
I am no fool
Love is the rule
I will make you cool
I will love you
I won't stop
When it's cool
Or when it is hot
I will hear your call
Don't worry at all
I'll love you
In the fall
We will see winter
Rain, chilly and cold
I will keep you warm
Through rain and storm
For all times
For heartfelt reasons
I will love you
All seasons

Soon We

Soon we
Will be together
Hooking up
Marrying you forever

Soon we
Will touch each other
Fall deeper in love
In bed undercover

Soon we
Will be one
Soon please
May the day soon come

Soon we
Will marry
Soon we
You and me

Soon we
Thinking of no other
Soon we
Loving forever

The Beauty of A Woman

It takes a
real man
to see the beauty
of a real woman
waiting at the DMV
a thought hit me
seeing the women
handle business / kids with duty
the smile of a
real woman
goes to the heart
of a real man
The nature of
A kind woman
Is a blessing
To every land
The beauty of
A woman
Lies in her
Nurturing hand
The beauty
of a woman
lies deep
in her kindness
The beauty
of a woman

Look into her soul
At her tenderness
Where you
will find
a woman
so kind

you will see
the real beauty
that makes a woman
a real cutie
a sister, daughter
or even a mother

Professional or a real wife
The joy of a man's life
A women's beauty,
A mother's sense of duty
And real integrity
Makes a woman a real cutie!!!

Nice Sister-Nice Day

As you are
On the way
You look so
Good Today!

In the sun's ray
I have to
Have my say!!
A day after
My 53rd birthday

As you pass
Me by
We meet
Eye to eye

I say
Hello or hi
You say hello
And walk by

Such a
Nice day
To see you
Smile my way

I salute my
Sister and say
Please Please
Have a nice day

Tribute To All African Women

This is a tribute
To all African-American Women
This is a tribute to All Black Women
You have always been
Our very best friend

Some think
We're not it
Some think
We're not up to it

Some think
We aren't
Worth it

This is a tribute
To all Black Women
You've always been
Our very best friend

Sharing our identity
Walking with us through history
Walking out of slavery
Sharing our destiny

This is a tribute
To all African Women
You've always been
Our very best friend

Together we are family
We are not enemies
We are together
Like birds and bees

Every time we spoke
We are the same folk
You are the best lovers
For me and my brothers

Never ever forget
Please unite us together
All of us
Are sister and brother

This is a tribute
To all Black Women
You have always been
Our very best friend

You are
A Work of Art
You are Queen of heart
You are
The roots we need
You are
The pillar of our creed

This is a tribute
To all African Women
Have always been
Our very best friend.

This is a tribute
To all African Women
This is a tribute
To All African-American sisters

This is a tribute
To all African sisters
This is a tribute
To all Black sisters

This is a tribute
To all Caribbean sisters
To all Nigerian Sisters
To All Ghana Sisters

This is a tribute to all Black Women
To all African women
You have always been
Our very best friend

Black Woman Dear

Black Women Dear
Please have no fear
Through good and bad
I'll always be near

Sisters get this clear
I'll will always be near
I will always be near
Black Woman dear

You are my mother
I'm your brother
my sister, friend or cousin
my love is overflowing

In the inner city
where we need more love
Even in the suburb
let peace shine down

Look and feel me
in your front
but I got your back
Black Woman like that

Please my sister
you have nothing to fear
smart and beautiful
Black woman dear

You are my love
You are my queen
Love you more than beer

Black woman dear
us together
let the vision be clear
you are my priority
Black women dear

I love it best
when you are near
I give you my heart
Black Woman dear

Keep me close
keep me near
I love you
Black woman dear.

Even More on Loving Black Women

There are some Black Women I have loved all of my life, like my beautiful Mother, who gave birth to my beautiful sisters, brothers and me.

Berdine Redd (my mom), Sharon, Sandra and Ann, my three sisters are Black Women I have loved and will continue to love as long as I live. I also have many relatives and cousins in the Bay Area, Los Angeles and around this country. All of my sisters, cousins and relatives are Black Women I have and will continue to love. I also have sister friends in Africa and throughout the USA that I have love for.

So you see I had to write some more after reflecting on the Black Women in my family, extended family and circle of friends.

My Mother has always been in my corner very compassionate, truthful and wise. We communicate very well and have always communicated even during challenging moments like when I first decided to wear my Afro up until today. I love my mother more than any words could ever say or convey.

My Mother is always there for me but also for all of her children. Mom believes in all of her children and grand children. Mom believes in all of us and sees our potential.

My sisters are all very beautiful supportive and intelligent. I love Sharon, Sandra and Ann. I love my brothers Darnell, Henry and Joseph. However this is a book about Loving Black Women.

I love my Father and my dad too, both the late Mr. Henry Redd, Sr. and the late Mr. Elijah Johnson. But again this book is about **Loving Black Women.**

I love my Aunties, Aunt Queen Ester and Aunt Dorothy. The pictures of my Mother and (her sisters) my Aunties, as well as some of my other female relatives are appreciated! .

I also loved my late wife Chinwe Amechi Uzoma Johnson-Redd.

I cannot say I love all my ex-girl friends, but I will say that I wish them all well.

Now that we have nailed down the foundations of my love for Black Women, let me say this about my new genre of poetry/ Spoken Word, Black love Spoken Word.

My Black Love Spoken Word flows from my heart like my love for my people. I have positive relationships with Black Women in my family including my late grandmothers.

About the Author

Larry Ukali Johnson-Redd was born in 1952 in San Francisco, he graduated from Balboa High School in 1970 and entered the University of San Francisco and received a B.A. in 1974 in Political Science and Ethnic Studies with an African American focus. His quest for education continued at Golden Gate University in San Francisco where he received a M.P.A. in Public Administration in 1976, and San Francisco State University whereupon he earned a M.A. in Educational Administration and an Administrative Credential in 2005.

During his early university days he met Chinwe, a Nigerian woman who was also a student, whom he eventually married. After being disillusioned by the racism encountered while seeking a career in corporate America, Ukali decided to seek alternatives. In 1977 he and Chinwe moved to Nigeria where he took a four-year appointment as a lecturer of Government at a Boy's High School in Benin City. While in Nigeria, he appeared on Nigeria Television on many occasions, wrote poetry and in his leisure time worked on his 1982 novel, *The Black Expatriate in Africa*.

In 1981 Ukali and Chinwe returned to the U.S., she subsequently developed health problems in 1984 and passed away in May 1985. Since then, he has mourned her, worked as a Community Services Executive in the OMI Community of San Francisco (twelve years), an elementary- secondary educator, and a High School principal in the Bay Area.

Ukali is also author of *Journey to the Motherland: From San Francisco to Benin City* (2002), and *History to Destiny Through Afrocentric*

Poetry (2003), and has made many appearances on Bay Area media outlets as well as produced many events. In 2005 he made a return visit to Nigeria wherein he was featured in the newspaper, and African Independent Television. For more information, he can be reached at 415-425-6711.

Loving Black Women is a different way of looking at the complicated nature of relationships: intimate or otherwise.

Johnson-Redd knows success. Maybe it's this optimism and faith in his community to reunite in love, irregardless present dynamics or the seemingly inextricable binds African people allow themselves to participate in which keeps men and women at odds. We are not trapped in these destructive paradigms is a message which shines through Johnson- Redd's text.

No matter how bad it gets... love Black women. The author writes again and again. Between these pages is work praising and loving what is good in African Diasporic sisterhood.

Loving Black Women shares the author's hope that other African Diasporic men will realize the loss to humanity when they forget to acknowledge, as Johnson-Redd has: "the beauty of a sister...."

Wanda Sabir
Arts Editor, *San Francisco Bay View Newspaper*
www.sfbayview.com
San Francisco, California

Amen-Ra Theological Seminary Press
10920 Wilshire Boulevard, Suite 150-9132
Los Angeles, California 90024-6502

LOVING BLACK WOMEN

is a two-fold book about realigning our awareness to the way brothers and sisters love each other and about over coming racial discrimination, political domination and white supremacy. I am not one to blush easily, but the author's Sweet lyrics in praise of everything beautiful, everything African and womanly, everything African feminine is at times Overwhelming.

Wanda Sabir, Oakland, Ca

Buy this book 2CD Audio Book $5..00
415-425-6711

http://www.youtube.com/user/ukalitheafrican
http://www.nathanielturner.com/larryuklaijohnsonreddtable.htm

Six Reasons To Read Journey To The Motherland From San Francisco to Benin City

*New price of Journey To The Motherland on Amazon.com $4.00 only plus shipping costs!

*New price on Loving Black Women (Audio Version only until Oct.1, 2010)

$5.00 only plus shipping costs. However Loving Black Women will also be released as a Kindle book very soon!

http://www.nathanielturner.com/larryuklaijohnsonreddtable.htm

*Link to Amazon.com is here: Go to this link and click on the image of the book or on the link to my page at the bottom of the table!

http://www.youtube.com/user/ukalitheafrican

1. Read Journey to understand how Africans particularly Nigerians viewed a brother in their midst from San Francisco, CA USA in the late 70's!

2. Buy this book to understand our ties to our African motherland and the cultural experiences of an urban African-American in Nigeria for a 4-year stay.!

3. Learn how the author's experiences will change your views on Africa! This book has a sequel type connection to Long Distance Love and is based on my experiences while living in Nigeria from1977 to 1981..

4. Buy this book and be transported to Africa while reading this book!

5. Buy this book to understand Africa better in the historical and contemporary basis!

6. Read this book that tells a positive Black story about a San Francisco born Black Man who graduates from 2 universities and travels to Nigeria, West Africa, our homeland for Africans all over the world. Once you read Journey To The Motherland give it to the Nigerian, Nigerian-American, African-American or West Indian-Caribbean you feel needs to read this book the most! A review of Journey To The Motherland by an African- American sister.

BOOK REVIEW by Veronica Brown Printed in the African Times Newspaper based in Los Angeles, California 03/17/03: Journey To The Motherland, From San Francisco To Benin City—Nigeria, written by Larry Ukali Johnson-Redd

If you are looking for some enlightenment, read this book Journey To The Motherland, From San Francisco To Benin City by Larry Ukali Johnson-Redd. It is a revelation of one man's insight and involvement in the political arena of racism towards Black students in this country especially in the 60'sand sadly to say still continues in today's society not only in the South but also in the West. The struggles, hardships they had to endure in order to obtain a decent education to better their lives in comparison to their white counterparts.

The first chapter opens with him and his wife returning from the motherland and in one solitude moment on the plane his thoughts flashes back to his youth in the city of San Francisco where he was born.

The next three or four chapters tell you of his days in junior and senior high school. His problems at securing a job was not with (out) its complications, event though his credentials were impressive and impressive they were however he persevered and conquered.

When both he and his wife accepted new posts in Africa, he as a teacher and she to work for the government, it was the most important decision any two people in love with each other could have made. For his wife, it was the best thing that could have happened because she was returning to her country of her birth and he was going there for the first time to his Homeland. The description of places and the cities he visited and most of all the people of Africa were awe-inspiring one only had to close their eyes and you can feel, hear and smell all the beauty and the sufferings that made Africa the great Continent she is and then you are suddenly transported there.

His description of family greetings, the meeting of old friends and the making of new friends and the making of new ones was something to treasure for a lifetime. While living in Africa he gives one the feeling that you never want leave once you get there, it was like coming home to heaven on earth, His time spent there was the most remarkable of his life with his wife along his side could not have completed a better picture. Much as he loved Africa, he still longed to be back home in America where his family still lived. He returned only to lose his wife and settled back to life in America.

Journey to the Motherland:
From San Francisco to Benin City

After being disillusioned by racism in corporate America, San Francisco born *Larry Ukali Johnson-Redd* and his Nigerian wife move to Benin City in Nigeria to seek new alternatives, whereupon he accepts a four-year appointment as a lecturer of government at a boys' high school.

In Nigeria the couple discover and re-discover personal and social challenges that are skillfully presented in a dream sequence that begins in the U.S. with the author as a student activist in 1967, and ends in the 1980's when he and his wife return to the United States.

The luminous autobiographical manifesto represents a continuing and progressive sociological exposé on the intersection and fluidity of cross-cultural understanding.

Journey to the Motherland is honestly rendered, making all the sentiments palpably real and strikingly descriptive of the people and idiosyncrasies of Nigeria. Ukali has made a beautiful effort to give flavor to where he has been, where he is coming from, and where he intends to go.

Adeyinka Fashokun, Ed.D.
Visiting Professor, Stanford Language Center, Stanford University;
Principal, Brenkwitz High School, Hayward, California

This work is a fantastic rite of passage story that places African social consciousness at the forefront of personal challenge, with dashing doses of reality. Readers will find *Journey to the Motherland: From San Francisco to Benin City* entertaining and culturally intriguing.

Itibari M. Zulu, Th.D.
Ralph J. Bunche Center for African American Studies at UCLA;
Provost, Amen-Ra Theological Seminary, Los Angeles

ISBN 0-9674226-3-9 $14.95

Amen-Ra Theological Seminary Press
10920 Wilshire Boulevard, Suite 150-9132
Los Angeles, CA 90024-6502

"Journey To The Motherland–From San Francisco to Benin City" Novel by Larry Ukali Johnson-Redd

Review By Kola Thomas

San Francisco, CA

This autobiographical "Journey To The Motherland" is a 160-page novel, but I read it in less than two days. Reading this book was an invocation of the nostalgia to be "at home right now."

This book is written in a style that helps the reader to be transported to Africa and be actively engaged in the dynamic and evolving events of the moment as they unfold. One could not help but follow the "Journey..." and soak in the moments. Perhaps being a Yoruba (born in Nigeria), familiar with the local terrain and socio-cultural manifestations and political landscape of Nigeria; and living in the Bay Area for over twenty-five years – well I travel home periodically - I am able to understand the book better. However, this is a book about a wonderful experience in Africa.

One thing that is clear throughout the book is a commitment by the author Ukali Johnson-Redd, to increasing empowerment for African people all over the world.

It behooves any one contemplating a visit to any part of Africa; to read "Journey..." A great many brothers and sisters go to Africa, without preparation or some form of orientation. They then experience cultural shock on arrival - shock at the mass of black people taking care of business; shock at the unparalleled and unqualified show of hospitality displayed by the hosts; shock at the high level of intellectual capacity and scholarship; shock at the fact that people are unfazed at whether or not utilities work; and shock at the fact that the urban and rural areas are just as any you will find in the so-called civilized western cities.

I could not help but be thankfully amazed at how Brother Ukali has assimilated the local lingo and nuances to a "T." Talk about "*invigilation...*" for proctoring a student test - page 124; and dispensing "*dongoyaro*" – a traditional herbal extract - as the preferred medication for malaria - page 144 - that follows age-long African understanding of traditional therapy – and which Western medicine refuses to celebrate. Perhaps Ukali needs to consider sharing his experience at medical colleges here in the United States.

"Journey to Motherland..." is recommended and a definite must read by every one who wishes to get a better understanding of Africa and African ways, its indubitable and welcoming hospitality, and its great culture, educational environment.

Kola Akintola-Thomas is CEO of African Global Institute-USA based in San Francisco, California. He can be reached at africanglobal@yahoo.com

If you missed this event the San Francisco Kings of Poetry Saturday April 10, 2010 or attended and enjoyed it do not worry a DVD will soon be available for purchase on my page at Amazon.com!!!

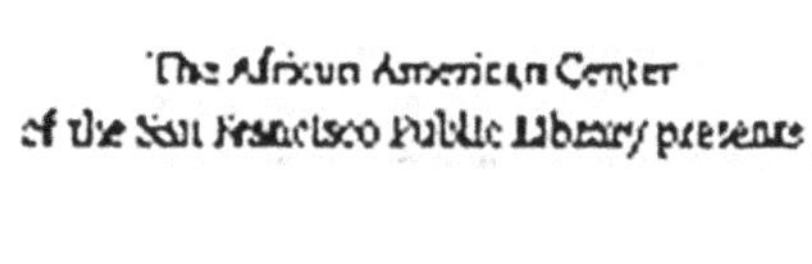

The African American Center
of the San Francisco Public Library presents

Kings of Poetry

Featuring:
Andrea Harris   Larry Ware
Larry Ukali Johnson-Redd
Terry Moore   Paradise

Saturday, April 10, 2010
2 p.m.
Main Library, Lower Level, Koret Auditorium

A poetry and spoken word event featuring African American poets
from throughout the Bay Area as well as an open mic session.

All programs at the Library are free.
Co-sponsored by Friends of the San Francisco Public Library

San Francisco Public Library

Main Library   100 Larkin St (at Grove)   (415) 557-4277   sfpl.org

134